A Note to Parents

P9-DNN-907

Reading books aloud and playing word games are two valuable ways parents can help their children learn to read. The easy-to-read stories in the **My First Hello Reader! With Flash Cards** series are designed to be enjoyed together. Six activity pages and 16 flash cards in each book help reinforce phonics, sight vocabulary, reading comprehension, and facility with language. Here are some ideas to develop your youngster's reading skills:

Reading with Your Child

- Read the st
  together. T
  Help your
- Read parts
  At first, pa
  Gradually,
  Then take
  book inde

Enjoying th

- Treat each
  to play.
- Read the i
  understan

Using the Fl

- Read the v
  and mean
- Match the
- Help your
  words tha
- Challenge
  the story

Above all el   that
reading is a   and
know that, a   ting
immensely to

Library of Congress Cataloging-in-Publication Data

Packard, Mary.
    The pet that I want / by Mary Packard; illustrated by John Magine
        p.   cm. — (My first hello reader!)
    "With flash cards."
    Summary: A boy has a very particular pet in mind, a dinosaur!
    ISBN 0-590-48512-1
    [1. Pets—Fiction.   2. Dinosaurs—Fiction.]   I. Magine, John, ill.
  II. Title.   III Series.
    P27.P1247Pe 1994
    [E]—dc20
                                                  94-16976
                                                  CIP
                                                    AC

12 11   7 8 9/9 0/0
                        Printed in the U.S.A.   24
First Scholastic printing, October 1994

THE PET THAT I WANT

by Mary Packard
Illustrated by John Magine

My First Hello Reader!
With Flash Cards

SCHOLASTIC INC.

New York Toronto London Auckland Sydney

The pet that I want

does not have fur.

It does not like to cuddle.

It does not like to purr.

The pet that I want

does not go tweet,

or carry a shell,

not	have
I	fur
the	does
to	that

through	want
cuddle	I
funny	feet
the	that

pet	or
like	dinosaur
a	it
is	tweet

fit	or
purr	shell
go	not
door	carry

or have funny feet.

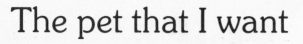

The pet that I want

does not fit through the door.

The pet that I want is a dinosaur!

The Pet That She Wants

The girl does not want a pet with feathers.

She does not want a pet with stripes.

She does not want a pet with a long neck.

She does not want a pet with fins.

Which of these pictures might be the pet that she wants?

Which Pet Did What?

Go back to the story.

Which pet likes to cuddle?

Which likes to purr?

Which goes tweet?

Which has a shell?

Pet Fun

Here are some pets doing many things. Which ones could be real? Point to them. Now point to the ones that are make-believe.

Time to Rhyme

Words that rhyme sound alike. Point to the picture that rhymes with the word at the beginning of each row.

shell

my

funny

like

The Pet for You

If you could choose one of these pets, which would it be?

Why did you choose that one?

Picking a Home for a Pet

Match each pet with its home.

Answers

(The Pet That She Wants)

(Which Pet Did What?)

cuddle purr tweet shell

(Pet Fun)

real:

make-believe:

(Time to Rhyme)

shell my funny like

(The Pet for You)   Answers will vary.

(Picking a Home for a Pet)

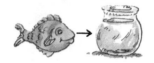